FOR LUCY SEKERS

First American edition published in 2006 by Boxer Books Limited.

Distributed in the United States and Canada by
Sterling Publishing Co., Inc.
387 Park Avenue South, New York, NY 10016-8810

First published in Great Britain in 1981
by Julia MacRae Books.

Text and illustrations copyright © 1981 Phillida Gili

ISBN 10: 1-905417-18-7
ISBN 13: 978-1-905417-18-6

Printed in China

The Lost Ears

Phillida Gili

Boxer Books

Once upon a time there lived a teddy bear called Harry, who was only two and a half inches tall.

He lived in Oliver's pajama pocket, where he felt warm and comfortable.

Nothing much ever seemed to happen to him, but he was extraordinarily well-read for a bear, because he could never resist reading whatever book Oliver was absorbed in.

He became an expert in farming,
knights and castles, dogs, birds,
trains, ships, deep-sea diving, and
dinosaurs, among many other things;
but he did long to read a story
that looked at life from
a bear's point of view.

Then one day something completely
unexpected happened to him.

Every week, Oliver's pajamas were
bundled up and thrown into
the laundry basket.

But this time Harry was
still inside the pocket.

A minute later he felt himself being
pushed into a dark hole, and
a door was slammed in his face.

He swam in circles for what seemed
like hours. The hot, soapy water
tasted disgusting.

Finally he was spun until he was
dizzy and then hung out on the line,
still in his pocket, feeling
weary and waterlogged.

He also felt extremely sick.
As he dried out he felt stronger,
but very, very annoyed.

Oliver's mother found him
when she ironed the pocket.

But oh dear! When Harry
looked in the mirror he had
a terrible shock.

He had lost his ears.

When Oliver saw him he said,

"That can't be Harry!

He looks ridiculous!"

And he put him away in a dark

cupboard with other broken toys.

Poor Harry thought his reading days

were over forever.

But a long time later

his inquisitive friend, Lucy,

came to play.

She opened the cupboard door.

"Oh, look at this sweet little

teddy bear!" she said to herself.

"Poor thing! All he needs is new ears.

I'll make him some right now."

She made them beautifully
out of felt. Later she made him
a red jacket, a blue scarf,
and a hat for cold days.

When Oliver saw Harry again,
he hardly recognized him.
He felt ashamed that he'd been
so unkind, and he put him gently
back into his pocket, where Harry
lived happily ever after.

Every week, Oliver made sure
to bring him books about bears
from the library, which pleased
him very much.